About the Author

Alexis Kincaid is a bestselling historical romance author! She's always had an obsession with reading factional stories about lovers from ancient times. Vikings are her favorite subject!

Alexis lives just outside of the Rocky Mountains with her husband, her bird/bat and mouse catching cat that has more adventures of anyone she knows, and her playful puppy. Before she started writing historical romance she dabbled in many fields, logistics, project management, home business but nothing felt like home to her until she decided to write her first Viking Romance and then it all fell together. This was what she was meant to do!

If you want to know when Alexis Kincaid will deliver another spell binding romance please visit here to sign up to get her newsletter letting you know of upcoming books and freebies. You can also follow Alexis on her Facebook page here.

Snowfall

A Viking Romance

By Alexis Kincaid

Chapter One

Fortress Vysala

Amid the chill of a winter's night, under the falling snow and the shifting trees, a babe was born, crying softly into her mother's breast. She was healthy and pink-cheeked, with a thin dusting of white-blonde hair atop her little head. As her pale-faced mother drew her last breaths, she ran a shaking hand through that soft, downy hair and called the child "Drifa".

That same child stared out of the tiny window, some 20 years later, and wished for her mother. It was a strange sort of ache-longing for someone she had never truly known, but it was there just the same. Her uncle had tried his best but he could not fill the empty space in her chest. No one ever would. Drifa sighed and her breath fogged, escaping into the world beyond the fortress. A familiar voice called her name from somewhere within the ample halls and Drifa turned from the window and made her way across the long room, her soft dress whispering across the rough floors. The fireplace had not been lit, here in the feast hall, and Drifa shivered in the chill. The heavy double doors creaked as she closed them behind her and she wrapped her arms around herself as she walked down the arched cloister.

There were torches lit throughout the open corridor, sending eerie flickering shadows dancing over the cold stone walls. Through the rough arches, the sloping courtyard of the fortress was washed white with new-fallen snow. Drifa walked quickly until she reached the huge, oak doors of the throne room. She pulled her fur cloak closer and pushed the doors open. There was soft laughter from the long mahogany table in the center of the room. The table had once been housed in the feast hall, she'd been told, but her uncle liked to take his meals in the throne room, which was quite possibly the warmest room in the structure during the winter months. A wide log in the enormous fireplace crackled and sent sparks drifting through the air. The windows were higher and smaller than those within the feast hall and Drifa was relieved to dins that she could no longer feel the chill.

Drifa's uncle Bjorn sat at the head of the long table, his broad, wool-clad back to the flames. There was a young dark-haired woman beside him. Drifa's cousin, Aada, sat laughing in the fur-lined chair just down from her father. They shared the same proud nose, thin and straight, though Bjorn's had been broken and left altered in battle. Bjorn's white-blonde hair contrasted with his daughter's and Aada's long braid glistened in the firelight. Drifa twisted a strand of her own white-blonde hair and curled the long tress between her fingers.

"Drifa!" Aada called, smiling widely. It was she who had called for Drifa, beckoning her into the throne room. Servants were spreading trays of warm food across the table. Drifa watched, her stomach growling, as they laid out platters of salted pork and steamy braised potatoes, honey-glazed root vegetables and smoked herring. There were round loaves of crusty brown bread in the center of the table and as Drifa took a seat opposite her cousin, a servant filled a tankard full of warm mulled wine for her to drink. She took it with sincere thanks and sighed as the aroma of their dinner fare wafted over to her.
"I've sent Inger to light your fireplace," Bjorn said, chewing on an impressive bite of salted pork. The scar across his right cheek pulled his mouth a little. "You really must remember to keep the hearth warm. You'll catch your death in this cold, child."

Drifa nodded, feeling a little chagrined. She *had* meant to ask someone to light it for her, only she'd forgotten once she realized the feast hall was empty and she could sit and think.

"I'll remember next time," she said unconvincingly. Bjorn let out a hearty laugh.

"You're so much like your mother. She would've forgotten her own hair if it hadn't been atop her head."

From the stories he'd told both she and Aada, he and her mother were as thick as thieves, running around the forest behind their childhood home with wooden axes and swords in their chubby little hands. Drifa's mother was a radiant memory. A blur of pale hair and hill-green eyes- a mixture of the imagined woman in her head and of her own face in her reflection. She died just after Drifa entered the world, leaving her only daughter in the hands of her trusted brother. Drifa's father was an empty face in her head. Her uncle never really spoke of him and the servants refused to tell her anything that Bjorn hadn't. She knew that he was a great warrior and was killed in battle just before her birth and that she had inherited his rather regal nose, russet brown eyes, and heart-shaped face.

"Were she and my mother friends?" Aada asked cautiously. They learned not to ask about her mother years ago, not unless they wanted to see that horrible, devasted look on her father's face, that is. He looked pained for a moment and dropped the potato he was holding onto his half-full plate.

"They yes- they were." He said haltingly. Aada's green eyes widened as she realized her father was going to reveal something about her mother. "I- your mother and my sister were very fond of each other. I believe Eira saved your aunt during a raid on her caravan and then she introduced her to me."

Lady Eira had been a tall, powerful shieldmaiden from the north. It was told that she swung a sword like no other and dropped men like they were nothing when they crossed her path. She died in battle, defending her men from invaders. She left behind one-year-old Drifa and two months old Aada in the care of her grieving brother, who had not long before, lost his brother in law and his sister in the span of a few days. He had moved them and the other members of their house here, to Fortress Vysala, then abandoned. Drifa took a drink of her rich wine, experiencing familiar respect for her widowed uncle. Aada was gripping the table with thin fingers, fighting the urge to ask her father more questions about her mother. Drifa watched her and took in the rosy cheeks, green eyes, and fine features of her younger cousin. She found it hard to equate the hardened warrior woman who was Aada's mother with the kind, soft girl in front of her.

"Any word of the raids in the east?" Drifa said, pulling off a portion of the fragrant bread. Inger had returned from lighting the fireplace in her chambers and she topped off Drifa's wine before any of the other servants could. She had been Drifa's nursemaid as a babe and they remained close through the years. Drifa nodded her thanks and realized she had effectively changed the subject. Bjorn looked relieved and Aada sat quietly in her seat, meticulously pulling apart a piece of fish.

"Many villages have been ransacked, families torn apart and children slaughtered in their beds. There must be hundreds of them, making their way across the countryside." Drifa's food didn't seem so appetizing after that and she stopped eating abruptly.

"But we're safe here, father?" Aada said beseechingly, her voice trembling. "They can't reach us within Vysala.?"

Whether it was his daughter's obvious fear that made him agree, or that they *were* actually safe within the fortress, Drifa didn't know. Bjorn took his daughter's hand and squeezed it.

"We are safe here, my daughter. We have guards and siege walls- they will not find us here. I will die before they take either of you." It was as if he spoke the promise into the room and the passage of time- bound his words like a covenant. Drifa was almost sure she felt them resonate through the air.

"You can lodge in my chambers tonight, cousin," Drifa told her. "I already have the fireplace lit." She winked at Bjorn and at Inger, who was standing behind him. They both laughed, winking back.

"Oh, Drifa," Aada said. "Are you sure?"

Drifa nodded and she too squeezed her cousin's hand. She liked it when Aada stayed with her. Their conversations, sometimes stretching late into the night, made her feel like she wasn't so alone inside the drafty, near-empty fortress. Bjorn clapped his head and pulled them both into a gigantic hug, laughing merrily.

They continued their meal in companionable silence and by the time their plates were empty and their bellies were full, the fire had crumbled into glowing embers and the chill began to creep into the expansive room. The servants began gathering the dinnerware and Inger pulled Drifa's cloak over her shoulders thoughtfully.

"You must wear a thicker gown, my love. More fur!." She inspected Drifa's thin wool gown and tsked, shaking her head. "This won't do. I'll have your garments lined with fur, not to worry."

"Inger, I'm really not that cold-"

"I won't hear it," Inger said, standing her ground. Drifa knew better than to question Inger's motherly affection. Bjorn stood up from the table, the silvery grey at his temples glimmering in the low light.

"Inger knows best," he shrugged, pulling his tunic up a bit to reveal the fur-lined interior. Aada did the same with her thick sleeve, grinning. Inger looked on proudly at them both.

"Oh, alright," Drifa exclaimed, throwing up her hands good-naturedly in defeat. Inger gave her a warm smile.

"I'll write in the order tonight," she said and promptly hastened them out of the throne room and out into the freezing cloister. Drifa heard her cleaning up and snapping orders at the other workers. There were guards stationed outside in the courtyard. Drifa assumed they were positioned all around the fortress, but she couldn't be sure. They must have been freezing though they didn't show it.

"I'll see you both in the morning," Bjorn said, rubbing his belly and cracking a yawn. "Get some sleep, we've nothing to fear."

He left them with a warm smile and turned toward in the direction of his chambers. Drifa and Aada made their way around the cloister and Aada raised an eyebrow as they passed the kitchens.

"Mead?"

Drifa grinned and suddenly in her excitement, the chill didn't feel so cold anymore. They snuck around the corner, on the lookout for Inger. She had caught them multiple times over the years and Drifa was determined to avoid her this night. Aada slipped quietly into the kitchens and Drifa heard her say "Aha!" very softly and she ran out with a sloshing jug of honey mead in her hands. They took off running and Drifa nearly tripped over her cloak in her haste to shut her chamber door. It closed with a creak and the two girls burst into elated giggles at their heist. Inger would eventually find them. She had a nose for alcohol, but they were finally in the warmth of Drifa's chambers and couldn't be bothered to care. They passed the jug back and forth until the smell of honey was on their breath and both girls were eager for sleep. In the morning they would join Bjorn for breakfast and then perhaps practice archery for a few hours on the overgrown training field behind the fortress. Aada wished her goodnight and Drifa was lulled into sleep by the sound of the wind outside and the popping and crackling of the fireplace.

Chapter Two

The Raid

Some time, deep into the cold night, Drifa awoke with a start. She had been dreaming of her mother, of the chill of death and decay. She could hear Aada beside her, snoring softly beneath the fur blanket. From the out of the high windows, there was only darkness and she wasn't sure what had woken her so abruptly. She made to lie back down against the down pillow and jumped suddenly as a shout rang out across the fortress. Aada stirred then, rubbing her eyes free of sleep and grumbling incomprehensibly. The fire still climbed high but Drifa shivered. She grew still, hoping the shout had been a servant or a guard barking orders for the night.

"Why did you wake me up?" Aada groused. "What's going on?"

"I didn't," Drifa replied, staring intently at the unlocked door.

"Drifa, what's happening?" Aada's voice had grown fearful at whatever she saw on Drifa's face.

"I don't-"

Drifa cut herself off as the large door burst open and someone came running in. Both girls screamed in terror and jumped from the bed onto the cold stone floors with their bare feet. Aada grabbed the mead jug and held it defensively and Drifa pulled out the tiny blade that she kept beneath her pillow. They braced for a fight, no matter their fear. The shape of a person grew clearer as the door was slammed shut and the firelight flickered over a harried face. Inger. Drifa thought she might cry in relief as she rushed forward to hug her nursemaid and Aada burst into tears behind her, dropping the empty mead jug onto Drifa's dressing table.

"Inger-"

"There's no time, my dear ones. They're coming and we must flee!" Inger grabbed their cloaks from the end of the bed and urged them to pull them around their bedclothes. "There's no time to change, we must go."

"Wait," Aada cried as she rushed them to the door. "Who's coming?"

"Vikings."

Drifa felt a jolt of fear run through her. She never imagined the raiders would travel this far south. Vikings were cruel, ruthless creatures who took what they wished and felt no remorse. She'd heard tell of them ripping animals apart and murdering those opposed them or kept them from what they wanted. Suddenly Aada's father came exploding through the door, sword in hand. There were two guards who followed him in. They covered in blood. He slammed the door behind them and looked at each of the women before him in turn.

"They've taken the outer walls, soon they will swarm the courtyard," Bjorn exclaimed, looking grave. He looked every bit the warrior he once was, standing in his tarnished armor with the glint of bloodlust in his green eyes.
They ran out into the cloister, huddling as close together as they could. There was a guard in front of their group and a guard behind them, watchful of their surroundings. Aada grasped Drifa's sleeve and they tried to move quickly and quietly passed the courtyard in out into wild landscape beyond. Drifa heard screams of terror rise from the keep and smoke billowed out from the gatehouse.

"The back entrance, through the old guardhouse," Inger muttered quietly. "It's the only way we'll make it to the stables."

Bjorn nodded in affirmation and turned to his daughter, holding her face in his large hands.

"Your mother loved you," he said, aggrieved. "I'm so sorry that I kept her memory from you. I wish we had more time."

Before Aada could respond, Bjorn turned to Drifa, "It's not the trinkets they're after Drifa, it's you."

"What? That doesn't make any sense." Drifa shook her head, looking to Inger for support. She wouldn't meet Drifa's eyes. The snow had begun to fall in earnest over the courtyard and Bjorn looked away from her as the entryway to the cloister was smashed open and dark figures streamed into the courtyard, holding blazing torches and glinting axes and swords. Bjorn leaned down to kiss his daughter's forehead as tears streamed down her cheeks. He glanced at Inger pointedly and she nodded fervently.

"Look after them," he told her. "Don't let them take her."

With that ominous statement, he hefted his sword and plunged into battle. The soldiers flanking their group followed him and Drifa watched them wade deeper into the fortress. Inger had them huddled by the archway and they hadn't been spotted yet. Bjorn had the advantage and he dove viciously into battle, cutting down three of the warriors within moments. Inger rushed the girls deeper into the open corridor, under the cover of shadow. Aada turned round again and again, hoping her father would be following close behind them after defeating his foe. Drifa turned and it seemed that time moved slowly in that horrible instant. All three of them watched as Bjorn turned to them, warmth on his face at having destroyed his enemies, then as if by the wrath of the gods, a sword stained with red pierced through his broad back and his armor fractured as the sharpened blade emerged from his belly. Aada screamed hauntingly and Drifa knew they were doomed. The tall man dressed in rough furs who had stabbed Bjorn jerked around at the sound and pulled his sword from his victim roughly. Inger pulled the girls while she cried silently, full of fear as the Viking made his way into the cloister. Aada attempted to go to her father but they pulled her back. The man grew closer to them, raising his bloody sword, and then fell suddenly onto his front, oozing crimson from the deep wound in his back. Bjorn watched them escape, still holding up the hand he'd used to throw the axe. He fell onto his side as they stumbled through the back entrance, his breath leaving his body.

Outside, the clawing cold bit at their cheeks and they shuffled through the substantial snow bank, down the hill in the direction of the stables. The fortress burned in the darkness, set ablaze by thrown torches. The screams from the dying had Drifa turning back, sick inside at the helplessness she felt.

"No!" Inger snapped. "We must get to the stables and leave this place, there's no helping them now."

Aada cried softly into her sleeve and Drifa wrapped her arm around her cousin's shoulders offering silent comfort, though she herself grieved at the thought of her uncle. She remembered what he told her and how it made no sense at the time and she was still struggling to understand.

"Inger," she said quietly as the raiders tore apart the fortress behind them. "What did my uncle mean before? Why would they want me?"

"Now is not the time, my love. I will explain it to you when we are all far away from here, deep into the shadow of the mountains."

Drifa was not content with her answer but they had reached the stables and she heard her horse call out, shrill in the night air. There were footsteps in the snow, far behind them and gruff voices grew closer. Drifa's hands shook, but she knew what she had to do. Inside the warm stables, her big bay mare stood, prancing anxiously in the hay beneath her hooves. Drifa rubbed her muzzle comfortingly. Inger and Aada lingered behind her. Aada reached her for father's horse, a black steed with thunderous hooves, but Drifa stopped her silently. Bjorn's horse was too obvious. He was the only black horse housed in the stables. Her cousin looked bewildered but the stress of the night had gotten to her and she climbed onto Alsvid without complaint. Drifa had forgone the saddle and Aada kept one hand buried in Alsvid's mane and the other on the thick reigns. Drifa motioned for Inger next but she narrowed her blue eyes in suspicion.

"Where will you ride?"

"I'll take Freya and catch up with you both," Drifa said, motioning to Aada's little sorrel gelding, quietly eating hay.

"I don't believe you, Drifa, what are you doing?"

Aada looked up at that, her dark eyebrows pulling together. Drifa cursed Inger's ability to always see through her lies. She had never planned on leaving with them. The men wanted her, right? She planned to let them take her with them and give Inger and Aada a chance to escape.

"Never mind Inger," Drifa shook her head like her nursemaid was just being foolish. "Here, I'll help you up."

"No-" The bolted stable doors banged open and raucous laughter filled the space with menace. Inger pulled Drifa behind her and Alsvid stomped her feet as Aada jumped, pulling at her dark mane. Aada looked absolutely terrified and Drifa was determined to keep her cousin safe. She made a decision then and winked at Aada.

"Ride hard and don't stop," without warning, Drifa smacked the flat of her hand against her horse's flank and Aada scrambled to stay atop her wide back. Alsvid reared and took off across the stables, barreling past the Vikings and out into the snow. Drifa watched as her horse's silhouette disappeared into the snowy night. Inger smiled at her and raised her chin, turning to the disgruntled men.

"I am Inger, daughter of Ingmar. If you wish to take the girl, you will have to kill me first."

"No!" Drifa cried, pushing around her nursemaid to stand tall before the raiders, her pale hair catching in the chill wind. "That will not happen."

There was a burst of deep laughter from the back of the group and a broad man moved to the front, his shadow flickering in their torchlight. Long, golden hair fell limp on either side of his noble-looking face, and braids that might neat once in his long beard had almost completely unraveled altogether. There was blood matted in the short hairs of his mustache and splattered across his face. He wore the rough fur and wool of his fellow warriors and a heavy axe was in his hand, intricate carvings on the handle and blade.

"Are you so eager to die for each other?" He said, his thin mouth quirking in amusement.

"Are you so eager to destroy lives and burn and take until there's nothing left?" Drifa replied, anger bubbling up inside her. She thought of her uncle and all he had sacrificed, and of their home, burning to meaningless ashes beneath the starless sky.

"I am Halvar, son of Rothgar," the man said, leaning his axe against the wall. "We've come to take you."

Chapter Three

Northmen

Throughout her short life, Drifa had only known a few people. She had been confined to the castle staff and to her family. There were no sleepovers with the neighbors or trips into town. Drifa had been isolated and she realized, as she bumped along with the Vikings, thrown on the front of Halvar's horse, that she liked it that way. The North men, as they were called, were barbarians. She'd watched them tear apart greasy slabs of game around the fire and lick their dirty fingers after, and then braid their beards and hair with those same greasy fingers. Inger was a few feet behind her, tied onto the packhorse so she couldn't get away even if she wanted to. Though Drifa doubted she would leave even if she could. She had pleaded with the fur-clad north men to take her with them as well and kicked up such a fuss that one of the big men, the one with the scar across his eye, had tossed her over the back of the horse and wrapped her in course rope. Drifa turned to look at her and Inger tried to smile, probably trying to comfort her, but it fell flat.

"Something wrong, milady?" Halvar said from behind her, mock-polite.

"Other than being captured by you and your disgusting brethren?" Drifa replied.

"You've been held by my disgusting brethren and me for a few days now so yes, other than that."

Drifa rolled her eyes. She thought about her poor uncle and her dear cousin, and then loyal Inger who could've been safe within the fortress Vikings had not been determined to capture Drifa, and wanted to cry so badly that she gripped the horn of the saddle until her thin fingers turned deathly white. Halvar shifted behind her but she paid him no mind.

"We'll camp here," he called suddenly to his men. Drifa looked around in confusion. Inger did the same. It wasn't yet close to nightfall and there was no reason to stop here. They were in the shadow of the mountains and it would be impossible to see someone if they wished to ambush them. Drifa thought for a moment and secretly hoped that someone would come and rescue her from the disgusting murderers who had taken her from her home. The rest of the North men began unpacking their horses with various levels of complaint and Halvar slid off the back of his bay mare, who flicked her elegant ears in response. He reached for Drifa who said "don't touch me," and jumped from the big warhorse with no elegance whatsoever. Halvar grunted a laugh. He turned and walked away from her, gathering wood to start a fire. Drifa stood huddled in the cold in her thin nightgown and fur cloak, shivering uncontrollably. She had been somewhat numb for the past few days and only thought about Aada, fleeing into the night, and she prayed to the gods that she was safe. Now though, the stress of the last week had begun to fall over her and her body felt light and she shook all over.

She reached for something, anything, to steady herself and the rough bark of a tree was under her hands. She stumbled past it and into the mountain forest, gasping for breath. She didn't know how long she lurched through the trees, unsteady and wishing so badly for her family, or even for her horse. She could hear Inger calling for her from across the small clearing where they were camped but Drifa could not go to her and she felt so very alone at that moment. She knew the North men would not bother Inger and so she kept walking. None of the other men tried to catch her and she supposed that they thought she was helpless and nothing to worry about. She found a tiny clearing where there seemed to be little snowfall and a where a thin stream coursed through, babbling softly over the rocks. Drifa slid into the cradle of a big tree's thick roots, and settled there, trying to breathe normally.

She watched a snowy owl race across the clearing and dive into the brush for a mouse. *I'm the mouse*, she thought sullenly. The moon appeared, bright and round, as the clouds parted. Drifa tipped her head back, leaning against the big tree behind her. She felt so weak. She had gotten not only herself, but her nursemaid captured as well, and there nothing she could do to stop the North men from taking her wherever they wished. There were footfalls through the forest, twigs snapping under heavy boots. Drifa froze. The steps grew nearer and she realized it must've been Halvar, searching for his captive. She rolled her eyes. Someone came around the tree then. It wasn't Halvar.

"What do we have here?" A nasally voice asked. It was a tall, dark-haired man, his body covered in scars. Drifa did not recognize him as one of Halvar's dozen or so men and she stood up from the tree quickly, heavy rock in hand. She pulled her cloak around her body and the man watched her hungrily, his eyes looking her over like his next meal. Drifa contemplated fighting but the man was much larger than she and there was no way she would be able to beat him. Without another thought, she took off running into the forest and she heard him grunt in surprise and follow her, his footsteps heavy. "Come back here!"

He grew closer and tears streaked down Drifa's cheeks as she struggled through the trees, trying in vain to reach the camp. She had only a moment to think how ironic it was that she was running to her captors to avoid being captured when a hand grabbed her ankle, yanking her onto the forest floor painfully. She gasped and the awful tried to flip her over but she fought, kicking him in his neck. He coughed in surprise and grabbed at his throat, gasping. Drifa slid away from him, grabbing another heavy rock.

"Stay away from me!" She cried. She could hear the terror in her own voice and hated it. The man stood up in a rage and went barreling for her, thick fist raised. He was only moving for a moment before someone flew into his side from the dark of the forest, knocking him down. Drifa recognized the golden hair. The fight was quick and saw the glint of a hunting knife come down on someone. She waited, barely breathing, to see who emerged. She was irrationally relieved and happy when Halvar stood from the wet underbrush, brushing off his damp doeskin trousers. There was blood splattered across his face and as he drew closer, Drifa saw a thin gash across his chest, bleeding sluggishly under his tunic. He paid it no mind and took a knee in front of her, his noble face earnest.

"Are you alright? Did he hurt you?" Halvar's eyes were blue and they shined bright like stars beneath the hazy winter moon.

"I'm fine," Drifa said, though she could feel herself begin to shake once again.

"We should leave this place; he can't be the only rogue."

"Rogue?" Drifa repeated, testing the strange word on her tongue.

"Men who have no loyalties but to themselves- usually men who have left their country's military and abandoned their cause."

There were more footfalls then, and Halvar slid rough hands beneath her and pulled her up, holding her in his arms.

"Let me down!" Drifa cried. She squirmed, uncomfortable at being held like a child. She could *walk*.

"Stop complaining," Halvar cried as he ran through the forest, jumping over the fallen trees and rocks. There were calls through the woods, rough cries and yells that grew farther away as the wind picked up. Drifa guessed that the calls were not from Halvar's men and she hoped fervently that Inger was alright, feeling awful for leaving her. The shock of her encounter with the man in the forest had worn off and Drifa wrapped her arms around Halvar's neck.

"Where are you taking me?"

"If those rogues find us, I won't be able to fight them all off by myself. We need to find somewhere to hide until my men come and find me."

"They won't know where you are," Drifa said.

"They know I went to find you," Halvar grunted, running through the trees. "Your nursemaid was making a fuss and threatened to kill me if I didn't find you, and just kill me in general."

Drifa smiled. "She would do it too."

"I don't doubt it."

The angry yells grew closer and Halvar stopped, looking around him desperately.

"There!" He exclaimed. There was a small opening hidden behind a thin grove of trees, a cave entrance. Drifa held on tight to him as he ran to the opening and grabbed a rock to toss it in, checking for animals. There was an answering silence and Halvar bent down a little, seemingly to make sure he didn't smack Drifa's head against the rock wall. It was dark inside, the only light shined barely visible at the entrance where the moon's glow fell over the cave floor. There was no way to tell how big or small the cavern really was and Halvar seemed cautious, sitting Drifa down gently. It was tall enough to stand comfortably inside for both of them. Halvar watched cautiously at the entrance as the sounds of the unfamiliar men grew close, and then let out a breath, slumping against the cave wall.

"This will do," he said, and Drifa watched the moonlight flicker over his face as he closed his eyes for a moment.

Chapter Four

The Cave

Drifa had always been fascinated by caves. As a child, she and Aada had made themselves sick with cold as they explored the small caves near the fortress, where all manner of forest creature dwelled. They had even seen a bear once, as they hid behind a wide tree, lumbering out of his cave and loping into the forest. Caves were magical to her back then, and there was a different world inside of each one. This cave, however, was not as much magical as it was damp and cold. Drifa paced back and forth and shivered, wishing for a fire. Halvar hadn't made a sound in several minutes and though Drifa was not necessarily fond of him, he had saved her life earlier. She paused and looked over at him. He was slumped against the wall with his legs stretched out and a sliver of moonlight caught in his golden beard, illuminating the strands. His eyes were closed and a ring of bruising had begun to form under the right one. His face looked vaguely kind to her at that moment and Drifa quickly shook away the strange thought. He didn't stir when she tapped his calf with her boot, and she thought for a moment and then kneeled down.

"Halvar..?" She said, unsure. She pressed a hand to his shoulder and her fingers came away wet with blood. She wiped it quickly on the lower part of her skirt and peeled his tunic away from the gash on his chest carefully. The long wound was worse than she had thought. It stretched from his left shoulder to below his right ribs and had soaked his tunic in the blood. He stirred as she tried in vain to put pressure on the wound. She could barely see inside the dim light of the cave and Halvar grabbed her hand and she turned away.

"Don't leave the cave," he said, looking tired. "I can't protect you out there."

"That wound is going to bleed our before your men can reach us."

"It doesn't matter," Halvar shook his head.

"Yes it does," Drifa snapped, and she realized oddly that it *did* matter to her whether he lived or died.

"No," Halvar said. "I'll be alright. My men will find you here and bring you to safety."

"Are all North men this stubborn?" Drifa raised an eyebrow.

"Only the ones with nothing to lose." Halvar grinned crookedly at her and her heart did a strange little jolt. She ignored it and made a mental note to ask him what he meant later. She was resolved and got up suddenly, determined.

"Where are you going?" Halvar said, sounding frantic.

"Yarrow," Drifa called back over her shoulder. Inger had been very thorough in teaching her the healing arts and though she hadn't listened to most of the lessons, rather more intent on going riding, she remembered how to clot blood with certain herbs.

After she had searched for an agonizingly long time, she finally found the flowers, half-dead from the cold, at the base of a tree. The snow was falling harder now and she could barely see through the white haze and into the forest. She ran back to the cave and found Halvar slumped onto the cold cave floor. She quickly flattened the hem of her nightgown and began crushing the flowers with a smooth stone. They were better dried and powdered, but this would work just as well. She pulled the water skin from Halvar's waist and poured it over the flowers, creating a soft paste. She tipped the water skin into his mouth and he coughed. Drifa rubbed the paste between her palms to warm it up and then gently pressed it into the wound. Halvar jerked and his eyes came open, blue and wild.

"It's okay," she soothed, trying to maintain a calm voice. Her hands shook on his chest with the cold and she could hear his teeth chattering. She needed a fire.

"I'm going to gather wood," she told him, though he probably wouldn't hear her.

He grabbed her hand with surprising strength as she turned to head back into the snow. "No fire, they'll find us," he said.

"It's a blizzard out there," Drifa replied in a placating voice. "No one is looking for us, good or bad."

She left before he could reply and she knew he was too weak to follow her. She would be hard-pressed to find dry wood with all of the damp undergrowth. Drifa remembered what her uncle had told her about finding dry kindling in a damp forest. She searched until she found a fallen log, its insides safe from the damp earth beneath. She reached cautiously and tore off hunks of dry wood, bundling them in her cloak to protect them from the falling snow. She gathered enough to last through the night if needed and then hurried back. She searched the cave for two rocks after she'd piled the wood up and then snapped the stones together until they sparked. She grew frustrated as she used the stones again and again and the fire remained unlit. A big hand covered hers suddenly and Halvar pulled the rocks from her hands. She watched him to be sure he was steady enough to sit up on his own and he leaned tiredly on her shoulder. He snapped the stones together once, twice, and then the flame caught and the fire began to climb in the kindling, warming the cave almost instantly. The snowy wind from outside caught most of the smoke and pulled it out into the night.

"Here," Drifa said. She had settled next to Halvar against the cave wall and began pulling hawthorn berries from her cloak pocket, distributing the bright red berries evenly between the two of them. Drifa popped all of hers into her mouth at one time while Halvar ate more slowly. He passed his water skin to her and she took a drink and handed it back.

"Thank you," he said, looking at his chest for the first time since she had spread the yarrow paste over the wound. She pressed his fingers experimentally to the edges and then winced at the pain.

"You're welcome," Drifa replied shortly. "Don't mess with it."

"I'm sorry about your uncle. I never meant for that to happen." He said, looking into the flames. " A Casualty of war."

"What war?" Cried Drifa angrily! She stood from the wall, as far away from him as she could without leaving the light of the fire. "We were living peacefully until you came along and destroyed everything." That brought her situation back into perspective and she realized with startling awareness that this wasn't some hero. Halvar had saved her for his own gain. There wasn't much he could do with spoiled merchandise and so he had kept her from the clutches of the rogue. This was a man who had in all likelihood, murdered hundreds of people and destroyed thousands of homes and had felt no remorse. Drifa turned away quickly, unsure of herself. She had saved this man too, nursed his wounds and fed him. What did that make her?

"I'm not who you think I am," Halvar said, sounding tired.

"Who are you then?"

Drifa had yet to turn around, even as she spoke, and Halvar made a soft sad sound like a sigh in the back of his throat.

"I don't know anymore."

"How about why you captured me, do you know that at least?" Drifa spun around, waiting. It was what she had wanted to ask since her uncle had told her that they wanted her and not the treasure.

"You should ask your nursemaid."

"I'm asking you."

"It's a long story and it's one I don't think you want to know, not really."

"Yes, I do. This may just be some mission to you, Halvar, but this is my life." Drifa fell to her knees in front of him, sick of asking others what she should already know. It felt like she knew nothing of her own life and the nothingness was suffocating.

Drifa almost jumped when Halvar's warm hand brushed over her cheek, as soft as the falling snow. His face had grown soft and he looked so very beautiful in the flickering light of the fire, the gold of his hair glowing warm and bright. Drifa wanted so very badly to lean in when he looked her over, his gaze lingering on her mouth. She needed him to say something, to do something to annoy her, so that she could remember why he was off-limits. He was silent though and he blinked slowly at her, moving the hand on her cheek to pull callused fingers through her pale hair. He raised his hand reverently to press over his heart, careful not to press against his wounded side.

"You're not what I thought you would be," Halvar murmured, tipping her chin and tilting his face into the angle. Their breaths mingled and Drifa felt her heart stutter.

There was something between them, something dormant that flickered to life like a lit candle wick when they touched. The drag of his hand over her skin was like the kiss of flame, hot and uncontrollable and she was loathed to ignore it. Drifa let their mouths press against each other for a moment and then she pulled away, unsure. At that moment he was all that existed- this man, war-torn and golden like the heat of the summer sun in the dead of winter. They shouldn't do this- *she* shouldn't. She never imagined lying with a man would be like this. She'd envisioned a lavish bed, goose feather pillows and the soft skin of an untested lord, handsome in the light of a dozen candles. Halvar's chiseled chest was scarred and tight, she pulled his shirt off gently, careful of his wound and she was mesmerized by the sight in front of her. He watched her as she traced her fingers over a dozen scars, a hundred marred points of tan, muscled flesh. Drifa felt a physical need she had never experienced before. She wasn't sure how it had come to this but she was too moved to stop it even if she wanted to. Drifa ran pale hands down the muscles of his belly and Halvar grasped at the fabric at her waist, looking up at her in question. She nodded and he gathered her nightgown in his hands and pulled it up, exposing her to the night air. Her nipples hardened as the air kissed her bare flesh. Her body had never felt this intense need before. She had never known this aching in her core, this desire to quench this thirst at any cost. The fire behind them turned their skin honey-golden and they seemed one being in the semi-darkness. Drifa shivered.

There was too much at stake, too much wrongness between them but she crawled into his lap anyway, instinctively tugging down his doeskin trousers. Halvar kissed down her neck, warm and wet, and Drifa threw her head back with a soft gasp. He looked up after a moment and she felt the thick heat of him beneath her. Without thought she reached out and took his member in her hands. She felt it from top to bottom then weighed it in her hands with fascination. Slowly she encircled it and started to move with the throbbing, gently up and down, her thirst grew as did his member. She was so engrossed in her actions that at first she didn't feel his fingers at her opening. She didn't feel them glide gently into her searching, probing up and around inside her until she almost exploded with pleasure. She looked down at how this could be, and saw his fingers sliding in and out at a pace she couldn't keep up with. She grew hotter and hotter and then mindless in a frenzy of intense pleasure that seemed to come out of nowhere. She gasped, she groaned she even screamed a little as she fluttered in and out of mindlessness.Oh Valhalla how had she not known this was possible?

He looked up and his eyes were burning, his want and need laid bare in his gaze. It was a question before they went too far before each of them was changed forever by the other. There was no reason to fight their feelings, their lust for each other here in the flickering darkness. Drifa nodded and they came together in a rush of breath and the mingling of their shared heat. Drifa winced at the pain of it and Halvar stopped for a moment and held her close, pressing their foreheads together. He would stop if she wished it and she could pretend she never knew the way he felt inside her and all around her. The thought of it was agonizing and she pushed his shoulder to keep going. Drifa felt awakened and brand new, forged in hot desire and shaped beneath warm hands. He started again slowly pushing deep inside her heat. Building his speed, she matched his thrusts over and over faster and faster until she could not contain herself any longer. Lights burst behind her eyes, her body shuddered uncontrollably, she screamed his name with passion then darkness came upon her.

A moment later she opened her eyes and felt him touching her face with tender care. "Ah my beauty you are blessed with a passionate surrender like no other" he whispered while kissing her face softly. "you make me crazy with desire. If I was not so injured I would take you over and over again, but alas our lovemaking has drained me of my last energy. Sleep little one." A soft smile appeared on her face as she closed her eyes but sleep was not to come.

They lay together, breathing softly. The shock had worn off and Drifa longed to pull away from him, though she wanted nothing more than to stay by his side forever. She tried not to think of what this meant. It changed nothing, though in her heart she knew that he would never again just be one of the North men to her. He had carved out a place for himself when he'd touched her skin and made love to her through the cold night.

"This is not something we can come back from," Halvar's voice was like a vow, made to the night and held in the moon's grasp.

Before Drifa could reply, there was a shout outside and Halvar sat up, tugging on his clothes. Drifa jumped away from him, her face growing hot. She pulled on her nightgown and stood, brushing herself off.

"One of your men?" She asked. He nodded. "Stay here," she said and left through the mouth of the cave. She pressed a hand to her heart to steady herself and tried to forget what had just happened and the things she had felt.

As soon as she stepped out, something smacked into her and she was engulfed in a hug.

"Oh, my little love, are you alright?" Inger cried, and Drifa could've wept at her nursemaid's familiar scent.

"I'm fine, Inger," Drifa said, squeezing her tight. "Halvar saved me from a rogue and we were caught in the storm. He's hurt."

The Northman with the scar across his face, Ragnar, stood behind Inger and when Drifa mentioned his liege lord, he ran to the cave that they had seen her exit. The other men were holding torches and she and Inger stood off to the side as a couple of men entered the cave and Ragnar and the others came out with Halvar strung between them. Halvar met her eyes and she looked away quickly.

"Find shelter," Ragnar said, in place of Halvar. "There is an abandoned settlement a few paces north of here. We'll go there."

Chapter Five

Blue Blood

The settlement was a few long buildings that resembled feast halls, and two smaller buildings, ramshackle and rundown. Nature had begun to take back what was hers and shriveled ivy climbed the wooden walls and curved around the corners of every structure. Ragnar led them inside the middle hall and the other men lit torches along the walls and braziers in the center of the room. The interior was almost entirely empty but for a few long tables and long-discarded weapons lying haphazardly around the room. The ceiling stretched high into the sky but the roof was thankfully covered and Inger helped Ragnar and the other men light a fire in the old fireplace at the head of the hall. Drifa was left to her own devices, close to where Halvar rested. She combed her fingers through her long hair absentmindedly and she could feel Halvar's blue eyes on her, strangely intense. She tried to forget the cave.

"Ask her," he said when she finally looked over at him. He was leaned up against one of the tables, a semi-clean cloth laid over his wounds. She'd watched them pour mead over his chest in disgust and then wrap his chest again after more yarrow had been applied. She ignored him and pretended not to care about him or his words. "If you don't ask her, you will always wonder."

"Not if you tell me," she challenged.

Halvar sighed, "It's not my story to tell milady-"

"Drifa." She snapped. There was no way he wasn't going to call her by her first name when she knew every single up-close color of his eyes and what his long, tan body looked like beneath his clothes.

"Drifa," he amended, smiling a little. "It's not hers either but there is no one else."

He looked at her soberly and she sighed, standing from the table. Inger was warming her hands in front of the fire. Drifa noticed Ragnar watching her nursemaid as he whittled away at a sharp piece of wood and saved the image for later when she might need it.

"Are you so opposed to telling me the truth?"

Inger looked up in confusion, her eyes going wide. The firelight flickered over familiar features and suddenly Drifa was a girl again, being rocked to sleep in her arms. She pushed the memory aside and waited, crossing her arms.

"Drifa-"

"No, either tell me or I swear to the gods that I will *never* speak to you again."

Inger looked pained but then the fight seemed to drain out of her and she gestured for Drifa to sit at the long table. The other men were busy and paid them no mind. "Your father was not a warrior," she started slowly. "Well, he was but he was also king- the greatest king to ever rule the north."

"King?" Drifa asked, her head spinning. There was no way.

"Yes, he was a kind and giving king and his people prospered under his rule. However, there was a leader rising beneath the guise of loyalty. Your father's right-hand man, his most loyal friend, gathered an army against him and staged a coup. Your mother had gone into sudden labor the king had no choice but to stay and fight. Those who remained loyal to him protected your father until the very end. He died protecting the nursery where your mother was giving birth. He heard the cries of his newborn daughter and saw your face for the first and last time that night. Your dear mother passed with your little hand wrapped around her finger and your father's right-hand man had him beheaded in the square. While the crowds were distracted, your uncle and I spirited you away from the fortress, under the cover of snow and nightfall."

"I'm- royalty?" Drifa could hardly believe it. She had always thought her father was a fallen warrior, not some warrior king, fallen from grace.

"Yes, my love," she said. "You were born to the north. Somehow the raiders found out where you were hidden and who you are. That's what your dear uncle meant."

Drifa stood up and stumbled away from the table, her heart in her throat. She had been lied to her entire life and everything had changed with one conversation. She walked quickly, anxious to get as far away from Inger as she could. Her nursemaid called to her but she ignored it, reaching the doors and opening them to a blast for chilling wind. She stepped out into the storm and the aching cold gave her something else to focus on. She didn't want to think about her dead mother or her father or her ancestry. She wanted to go home, to her uncle and to Aada and Alsvid. But there was nothing left to go home to and that life had been a lie anyway. She wanted to take off into the snow and never look back. She wanted to go somewhere that no one knew her and she could forget about her past. The door opened and Halvar came to her, hunched over from the cold and his wound.

"Go back inside," Drifa snapped.

"I'm the leader of this company, remember?"

Drifa turned on him, getting as close as she could to be heard over the howling wind.

"And I'm the princess," she said, challenging him to correct her.

"He's my father," he said instead and Drifa stared at him, waiting for him to explain.

"The one who betrayed the king- it was my father."

"You-" Drifa started, vibrant with rage. "You're taking me to him, aren't you? Like a sow to the slaughter."

She wanted to slap him. She wished she had left him in that cave, bleeding out on the cold, damp stone. He had touched her and changed her and she had let him. She felt hurt and strange betrayal flash through her all at once.

"No- yes," Halvar said, shaking his head. Drifa watched his muscles move beneath his ripped tunic and saw the pale bandage peak from underneath. "But now I don't- my father told me that your whole family was cruel, that they were tyrants and that your father's continuous tax on simple farmers and peasants had led to kingdom-wide poverty while your family gorged themselves on foreign foods and lavish wines. But you- you're kind and fair and you have the heart of a warrior, as brave as any of my men, saving your cousin and sacrificing yourself like that. And then you saved my life when you could've left me to die and escaped into the night. You could've left so easily. Why did you stay? Tell me-"

Drifa pulled him down by his beard and kissed him, relishing the warmth of his mouth on hers and the tickle of his mustache. His mouth tasted of mead and he wrapped an arm around her back, pulling her closer. It felt right, to be so close to him again. She pressed a hand to his chest after a moment and he pressed his forehead against hers before pulling away.

"I'm leaving," Drifa said softly and didn't care if he couldn't hear her over the wind. "Inger and I are going and you won't stop us."

Halvar looked at her for a long moment, something unknown in his eyes and then he nodded. "I'll tell my father you got away from me and it will be the truth." He let her pass and she found Inger, sitting quietly by the fire. Ragnar was next to her and they both looked up when Drifa came closer.

"My little love I'm so-" Inger started.

"We're leaving," Drifa said shortly. Inger looked confused but she could feel Halvar behind her and he must've nodded or something similar because Ragnar handed Inger a carving and stared at her before nodding. The other men watched them as they made their way across the hall. Halvar stopped Drifa with a hand on her arm, his blue eyes pleading.

"You must be careful; there are others who know now."

Drifa nodded and pressed a hand lightly to his chest, "keep this clean and don't strain yourself."

Halvar looked like he wanted to say something else but he only stared, watching she and Inger leave through the double doors without a goodbye.

Chapter Six

Mikkel

Drifa and Inger walked until they found the cave that had been she and Halvar's safe haven and they stayed there for the night. In the morning, the storm had cleared but the snow was deep.

"We must find horses," Drifa said. Inger agreed and they set off to find a town or a villager whom they might barter with for a steed. Inger had a small pouch sewn into her cloak with jewelry and coins from the fortress and soon enough, they came upon a small farm. Drifa offered the farmer four coins for his strong young plow horse and the farmer took the money gratefully, exclaiming that he could buy three horses with that kind of money.

Drifa and Inger rode he horse bareback so there would be less weight and both of them could ride. They walked until the snow thinned and Drifa could just make out the North Sea through the dense trees. They stopped at a small ravine and let the horse drink and eat his fill of the old, summer grass by the bank. Drifa found a few mushrooms and some hawthorn berries and they ate on their cloaks, relieved at the chance to rest. She could feel Inger looking at her and she turned from where she had been staring at the big horse. He reminded her of her uncle's steed.

"Do you want to tell me what happened with Halvar, why he let us go? I think I can guess."

Drifa sighed, almost too tired to talk, "he is the traitor's son."

"I know."

"You *know*?" Drifa looked at her in disbelief.

"Rothgar was a handsome man and his son looks almost exactly like him. I was hoping he was not like him in his manner and I was right."

"I don't know what to think of him, or of myself. I don't even know who I am anymore, Inger."

"Oh my love," Inger cried, sounding close to tears. "You are Drifa and that hasn't and won't ever change. You are your mother's joy and your father's pride. You are the greatest gift I ever received."

Drifa turned to her and let all of her anger and hurt fade as she threw her arms around her nursemaid and held on tight.

They left the clearing and the forest thinned into grassy plains stretching all the way to the sea. Drifa saw herself and Inger boarding a ship and never returning. There were boats docked down below, their sails white against a brilliant blue sky. Drifa urged the horse into a soft gallop and as they crested the hill, she noticed another party, traveling quickly in their direction. Drifa tried to turn the horse back the way they had come and Inger cried out that they needed to leave but it was too late. The party was upon them. Their horses wore colorful crests and their saddles tinkled with tiny bells. This was no warrior party or hunting faction. Their attire told of the pomp and decadence of court life. A tall, gangly man dismounted from his lovely white horse and threw his hands out in greeting. He was handsome, the way that coins were shiny or jewels glittered. His body was long and lean and his thin beard was shaved clean, a far cry from Halvar and his warriors.

"My princess," he said. Drifa frowned as he bowed. "Allow me to introduce myself. I am Lord Mikkel, son of Rodolphus. I am your betrothed."

"Mikkel?" Inger said, looking at him in suspicion. "I thought your family turned traitor during the war. Rodolphus let the soldiers in the west gate, causing the coup."

Mikkel looked peeved, "my dear father has realized the error of his ways and sent me to collect you, my love. We are to be married on the morrow."

"No-!" Inger started.

"What right do you have to tell me what to do or where to go? I don't even know you. I'm not going anywhere with a traitor." Drifa interrupted.

"My dear," Mikkel said loudly. "Be very careful how you use that sharp tongue, or else one day you might find it cut from your mouth."

"Touch her and you die where you stand," as a strong, familiar voice called. Drifa's heart beat quickly and she turned to see Halvar and his men raving over the hill on horseback, their weapons raised. They were akin to the great warriors of legend, arriving at the battle just when they were needed most. It had only been a few days but Halvar looked better, though he still curled into his side a little. The North men surrounded Mikkel's party, whose tiny pretty horses and bright clothing looked laughable next to their warhorses and furs.

"And who are you, barbarian?" Mikkel sniffed haughtily. He put his hand on the thing sword hilt at his side, as if he were trying to appear threatening.

"Put that letter opener away before you hurt yourself, little boy," laughed an older warrior. Drifa thought his name was Lothar.

"Little boy-!" Mikkel cried, outraged. "I'll have you know, I am the son of Lord Rodolphus of the western isles and I will not be treated in this manner! I will take the girl and leave-"

"No one takes her but me," Halvar said, looking at Drifa for a moment. Drifa smiled.

Mikkel looked confused and agitated. He was about to say something else but Ragnar made a sound to get his attention.

"Tell your father that Princess Drifa is under the protection of the men of the north and leave this place, or lose your head."
Mikkel looked back and forth between all of them and huffed, taking long strides and pulling himself back up in his embroidered saddle.

"This isn't the end," he said, trying his best to appear imposing.

"It will be for you if you don't leave now," Halvar said, raising his eyebrows. Drifa had to fight the urge to laugh as Mikkel hurried to turn his party around, headed back in the direction that he came. How Drifa's father could ever have her engaged to a man like that, she didn't know. Inger slid from their horse and Ragnar pulled her up behind him, talking softly. Drifa urged her horse closer to Halvar and he looked back ar her as he put his broadsword away.

"Captor to savior, huh?"

Halvar snorted, "I regret the first one."

"Why did you follow me? What will your father say?"

"I don't know. He will be angry but I can't risk you." Drifa felt her face soften at that and she pressed a hand to his bearded cheek for a moment.

"Where to?" Lothar said, scratching at his greying beard.

Drifa thought for a moment and then looked out at the water and the Cliffside. "The sea," she said.

Chapter Seven

The North Sea

It was a short ride to the Cliffside and they arrived with little fanfare. They guided their horses down the steep embankment to where the longboats were docked and dismounted once they had reached the bottom. There were people here and there, seamen returning from the open water and farmer's loading their crops to be sold across the water. Inger and Ragnar managed passage on a merchant's vessel with a small crew. Halvar loaned a few of his men that were willing to work for the price of taking them all safely across the sea. They let their horses go and Drifa hoped the plow horse that had saved them days of walking would find his way back to his owner. The vessel was getting ready to sail and Drifa sat in the cold sand on the beach with the hood of her cloak pulled up. A figure sat down heavily beside her and Halvar's voice said,

"Are you okay?"

After all that she had been through and all that she had learned and all of the troubles that she was trying to escape, she could honestly say that she was. She was alive and salvation seemed so very close. She nodded, tugging her hood down.

"How's the chest?"

"Better," he replied, rubbing absentmindedly at the fresh bandages there.

"Thank you for saving me earlier, Halvar, I don't know what-"

An arrow flew through the air and smacked into the chest of the merchant, killing him instantly. Halvar stood up quickly, putting himself between Drifa and immediate danger. A host of men, dressed similar to Halvar's warriors came charging down the hill, their weapons raised. Once Drifa got a good look at Halvar's face, she realized he was afraid. She stared at the men and pulled the hunting knife from Halvar's waist, ready for battle. She was surprised when Halvar's men did nothing and then she realized that they knew the other party. A man who looked almost exactly like Halvar, but with line of age, jumped down from his horse. He looked around at them all, his eyes landing on Drifa for the longest and then at Halvar's arm, raised to protect her. The man that had to be Rothgar narrowed his black eyes and Drifa had the urge to place herself in front of Halvar, to shield him from his father.

"My son," Rothgar said. His voice was deep and resonating. Many of Halvar's men had gone to his father's side. Only Ragnar, Lothar, and two young warriors remained. "I was under the impression that you lost the girl. I suppose what you really lost was your head." He said it mockingly, dripping with ridicule.

"We're leaving father, there's nothing left for you to do." Halvar stood strong and didn't tremble or stutter as he spoke the words, but his sword hand twitched like he was itching for battle or to throw the weapon down, either way. Drifa gripped his other hand. Rothgar turned to where Inger and Ragnar stood, close but not touching.

"Hello dear Inger, how was it in seclusion?"

Inger made a nasty face and said, "a hundred years in solitude would be preferable to mere minutes in your presence, dear Rothgar."

Rothgar threw his head back and laughed heartily. "You didn't seem to think that way twenty years ago, my old love."

Drifa looked over at Inger in shock. He was lying, wasn't he?

"Or when you told me which doors would be easier to sneak a couple of hundred soldiers in to," he continued, looking smug. Drifa gasped. Inger's face grew red and Ragnar put a hand on her back.

"I had no idea what you were planning, you bastard!"

"Yes well," Rothgar said, dismissing her words with a wave of his hand. "Now you," he said, finding Drifa's face in the crowd. "You are a lovely creature, so much like your mother in that aspect. It's a shame she passed, such a waste of a beautiful woman."

Drifa gripped her knife hard. "I won't go with you."

"Aw but that stubbornness comes from your father-"

"If anything else about either of my parents leaves your traitor mouth again, I'll slit your throat," Drifa said, her voice hard, serious in every word. Even Halvar looked down at her in surprise.

"Well, you've been forged in flame, little one," Rothgar whistled, looking impressed. "I would be interested to know what kind of wife you would make."

Everyone at the docks voiced their shock and Halvar said: "father you can't mean-"

"What did you think I wanted her for, son?" Rothgar laughed. "She's of royal blood, our brood would be of royal standing and no one would doubt my kingship then."

Without another word, Halvar rushed his father, raising his sword. Rothgar was quicker and he blocked the attack. They fought, throwing powdery sand into the air and drawing blood. Halvar was ferocious like he wanted to tear his father apart. They fight came to a head and Halvar had his blade against his father's throat. Out of the corner of her eye, Drifa saw one of the bowmen raise his crossbow. Ragnar cried "no!" and leaped into the fighting, pushing Halvar off into the sand. King Rothgar's throat was cut and his men stood around him, watching rose-red spread around him in the pale sand.

The warriors looked up at Halvar after a moment and each knelt in turn, bowing to the new king in the north. Halvar shook his head. He would never be what his father was and he urged the men to rise. All around him, they were bowing and pledging their fealty to him. "The king is dead, long live the king!" They intoned, stabbing their swords into the sand. Halvar turned his attention to the scene before him. The people at the docks came out from their hiding spots and Drifa rushed over to hear Inger scream in grief. Ragnar had taken the arrow for Halvar and lay bleeding in the sand. Inger pulled him up onto her lap and whispered softly to him, clutching the whittled trinket he had made her in her hand. Drifa fell into the sand, desperate to save him. Halvar was bent over him and he waited with bated breath as Drifa looked him over. Tears streaked down her cheeks and she shook her head,

"I'm so sorry, Ragnar," her voice shook and Halvar bent over his friend, holding one scarred hand in his.

"Thank you, old friend. What can I do?" Halvar said with his voice breaking.

"Live your life and love your woman," Ragnar intoned, kissing Inger's palm one last time before succumbing to his wound. Halvar laughed wetly and gripped his hand hard as he faded and his eyes closed for the last time. Inger cried over his body even as the others had laid him in a small boat filled with trinkets and herbs. Drifa pulled her back onto the shore as they watched Ragnar's body disappear into the waves. One of the archers lit a flaming arrow and it whistled through the air, catching fire as it reached the boat. Inger sobbed into her shoulder and they all shuffled silently onto the ship. Halvar looked back once at father's body as his (now Halvar's) men carried him back up the embankment and then no more. He'd instructed them to take his father to the funeral pyre at the fortress and did not much care what happened to him after.

"Well," he said "Where to now, princess?"

Drifa laughed, her pale hair catching in the wind. For the first time, she felt almost free, and said, "I suppose we have a kingdom to restore, if you are up to it my love".

Liked this story? Then stay tuned as we follow Aada's adventure in the next book Coming soon!

Want more books like this one sign up for our free newsletter here and be the first to hear of our next books, get some freebies, and join upcoming reader contests.

Make Tonight a Sesso Dolce Night!

With Sesso Dolce, the arousal happens very quickly, usually within minutes. It's your organic and safe solution to dramatically increase pleasure during intimacy.

- Deeply intensifies romantic sensations

- Increases lubrication naturally

- Increases intensity and passion

Order Here: www.sessodolcenight.com